THE LAYING ON OF HANDS

THE LAYING ON
OF HANDS

A STORY BY

Alan Bennett (signature)

ALAN BENNETT

P

PROFILE BOOKS
in association with
LONDON REVIEW OF BOOKS

First published in book form in Great Britain in 2001 by
PROFILE BOOKS LTD
58A Hatton Garden, London EC1N 8LX
www.profilebooks.co.uk

First published in 2001 by
LONDON REVIEW OF BOOKS
28 Little Russell Street, London WC1A 2HN

This paperback edition first published in 2002

1 3 5 7 9 10 8 6 4 2

Typeset in Quadraat
Designed by Peter Campbell
Printed and bound in Great Britain by
St Edmundsbury Press, Bury St Edmunds

A CIP catalogue record for this book is
available from the British Library.

ISBN 1 86197 426 4

S EATED OBSCURELY towards the back of the church and on a side aisle, Treacher was conscious nevertheless of being much looked at. Tall, thin and with a disagreeable expression, were this a film written forty years ago he would have been played by the actor Raymond Huntley who, not unvinegary in life, in art made a speciality of ill-tempered businessmen and officious civil servants. Treacher was neither but he, too, was nothing to look at. Yet several times he caught women (and it was women particularly) bending forward in their seats to get a better view of him across the aisle; a murmured remark passed between a couple in front, the woman then turning round, ostensibly to take in the architecture but actually to look at him, whereas others in the congregation dispensed with such polite circumspection and just stared.

Unwelcome enough in any circumstances, this scrutiny was not at all what Treacher had had in mind when he had come into the church fully half an hour before the service was due to start, a precaution against having his hand shaken at the door by the vicar. Such redundant clerical conviviality was always distasteful to Treacher but on this occasion he had a particular reason for avoiding it. Luckily the vicar was not to be seen but, early as he was, Treacher had still had to run the gauntlet of a woman in the porch, a reporter presumably, who was making a record of those attending the memorial service. She held out her book for him to sign.

'Name and organisation?'

But Treacher had pushed past as if she were a lowlier form of autograph hunter. 'Not important,' he said, though whether he meant he was not important or that it was not important his name be recorded was not plain.

'I'll put you under "and many other friends",' she had called after him, though in fact he had never met the deceased and did not even know his name.

Somewhere out of the way was what he wanted, where he could see and not be seen and well back on the side aisle he thought he had found it, instead of which the fuller the church became the more he seemed the focus of attention. It was very vexing.

In fact no one was looking at Treacher at all, except when they pretended to look at him in order also to take in someone sitting in the row behind. A worldlier man than Treacher, if worldliness consists in watching television, would have known why. Seated behind him was a thick-set shaven-headed young man in dark glasses, black suit and black T-shirt who, minus the shades and occasionally (and far too rarely some viewers felt) minus the T-shirt, appeared nightly on the nation's screens in a television soap. The previous week he had stunned his audience when, with no excuse whatsoever, he had raped his mother, and though it later transpired she had been begging for it for some time and was actually no relation at all, nevertheless some vestiges of the nation's fascinated revulsion still clung to him. In life, though, as he was at pains to point out to any chat-show host who would listen, he was a pussy-cat and indeed, within minutes of the maternal rape, he could be found on another channel picking out the three items of antique furniture he would invest in were his budget limited to £500.

None of this Treacher knew, only becoming

9

aware of the young man when an usher spotted him and insisted on shepherding the modest hunk to a more prominent seat off the centre aisle next to a chef who, though famously disgruntled in the workplace, now smilingly shifts along to accommodate the big-thighed newcomer. After his departure Treacher was relieved, though not unpuzzled, to find himself invisible once more and so able to look unobserved at the incoming congregation.

There was quite a throng, with people still crowding through the door and a small queue now stretching over the worn and greasy gravestones that paved this London churchyard. The flanks of the queue were harried by autograph hunters and the occasional photographer, outlying celebrities meekly signing as they shuffled on towards the door. One or two did refuse, on the justifiable grounds that this wasn't a first night (and more of a closing than an opening), but the autograph hunters were impatient of such scruples, considering themselves wilfully thwarted. 'Choosy cow,' one muttered as he turned away from some glacial TV newsreader, brightening only when he spotted an ageing disc jockey he had thought long since dead.

The huddled column pressed on up the steps.

As memorial services go these days it had been billed as 'a celebration', the marrying of the valedictory with the festive convenient on several grounds. For a start it made grief less obligatory, which was useful as the person to be celebrated had been dead some time and tears would have been something of an acting job. To call it a celebration also allowed the congregation to dress up not down, so that though the millinery might be more muted, one could have been forgiven, thought Treacher, for thinking this was a wedding not a wake.

Clive Dunlop, the dead man, was quite young – 34 according to the dates given on the front of the Order of Service, though there were some in the congregation who had thought him even younger. Still, it was a shocking age to die, there was no disagreement about that and what little conviviality there might have been was muffled accordingly.

Knowing the deceased, many of those filing into the church in surprisingly large numbers also knew each other, though in the circumstances prevailing at funerals and memorial services this is not always easy to tell as recognition tends to be kept to a minimum – the eye downcast, the smile on hold, any display of pleasure at the encounter or even shared grief postponed until the business of the service is done – however sad the professionally buoyant clergyman will generally assure the congregation that that business is not going to be.

True, there were a number of extravagant one-word embraces, 'Bless!' for instance, and even 'Why?', a despairing invocation that seemed more appropriate for the actual interment which (though nobody seemed quite to know where) appeared to have taken place some six months previously. Extravagant expressions of sorrow seemed out of place here, if only because a memorial service, as the clergyman will generally insist, is a positive occasion, the negative side of the business (though they seldom come out baldly with this) over and done with at the disposal of the body. Because, however upbeat a priest manages to be (and indeed his creed requires him to be), it's hard not to feel that cheerful though the memorial service can be, the actual interment does tend to be a bit of a downer.

Still, discreet funerals and extravagant memorial services are not unusual these days, the finality of death mitigated by staggering it over two stages. 'Of course there'll be a memorial service,' people say, excusing their non-attendance at the emotionally more demanding (and socially less enjoyable) obsequies. And it is generally the case nowadays that anybody who is anybody is accorded a memorial service – and sometimes an anybody who isn't.

Hard to say what Clive was, for instance, though taking note of the numerous celebrities who were still filing in, 'well-connected' would undoubtedly describe him.

Dubbing such a service a celebration was, thought Treacher, a mistake as it could be thought to license a degree of whoopee. The proceedings seemed to include a saxophone solo, which was ominous, and Treacher's misgivings were confirmed when a young man sat down heavily in the pew in front, laid his Order of Service on the ledge then put his cigarettes and lighter beside it.

She was in the next pew, but spotting the cigarettes the spirits of a recently ennobled novelist rose. 'You can smoke,' she whispered.

Her companion shook her head. 'I don't think so.'

'I see no signs saying not. Is that one?'

Fumbling for her spectacles she peered at a plaque affixed to a pillar.

'I think,' said her friend, 'that's one of the Stations of the Cross.'

'Really? Well I'm sure I saw an ashtray as I was coming in.'

'That was holy water.'

In the light of these accessories, more often to be met with in Roman Catholic establishments, it was hardly surprising if some of the congregation were in doubt as to the church's denomination, which was actually Anglican, though a bit on the high side.

'I can smell incense,' said a feared TV interviewer to his actress friend. 'Are we in a Catholic church?'

She had once stabbed a priest to death in a film involving John Mills so knew about churches. 'Yes,' she said firmly.

At which point a plumpish man in a cassock crossed the chancel in order to collect a book from a pew, bowing to the altar en route.

'See that,' said the interviewer. 'The bowing? That's part of the drill. Though it looks a bit pick 'n' mix to me. Mind you, that's the trend these days. Ecumenicalism. I talked to the Pope about it once. Sweet man.'

'I missed the funeral,' whispered one woman to her vaguely known neighbour. 'I didn't even know it had happened.'

'Same with me,' the neighbour whispered back. 'I think it was private. What did he die of?'

The sight of a prominent actor in the Royal Shakespeare Company gliding humbly to an empty place in the front row curtailed further discussion, though it was the prototype of several similar conversations going on in various parts of the church. Other people were trying to recall why it was they had failed to attend a funeral which ought to have been high on their lists. Was it in the provinces they wondered, which would account for it, or one of the obscurer parts of South London . . . Sydenham, say, or Catford, venues that would be a real test of anybody's friendship?

It had actually been in Peru, a fact known to very few people in the congregation though in the subdued hum of conversation that preceded the start of the service this news and the unease it generated began to spread. Perhaps out of tact the question, 'What did he die of?' was not much asked and when it was sometimes prompted a quizzical look suggesting it was a question best left unput; that, or a sad smile implying Clive had succumbed not to any particular ailment but to the general tragedy that is life itself.

Spoken or unspoken, the uncertain circumstances of the death, its remote location and the shocking prematureness of it contributed to an atmosphere of gloom and, indeed, apprehension in the church. There was conversation but it was desultory and subdued; many people's thoughts seemed to be on themselves. Few of them attended a place of worship with any regularity, their only contact with churches occasions like this, which, as was ruefully remarked in several places in the congregation, 'seemed to be happening all too often these days'.

To Treacher, glancing at the details on the front of the Order of Service it was all fairly plain. He was a single man who had died young. Thirty-four. These days there was not much mystery about that.

'He told me 30, the scamp,' said one of the many smart women who was craning round to see who was still coming in. 'But then he would.'

'I thought he was younger,' said someone else. 'But he looked after himself.'

'Not well enough,' said her husband, whose wife's grief had surprised him. 'I never understood where the money came from.'

Anyone looking at the congregation and its celebrity assortment could be forgiven for thinking that Clive had been a social creature. This wasn't altogether true and this numinous gathering studded with household names was less a manifestation of his friendships than an advertisement for his discretion.

It was true that many of those present knew each other and virtually all of them knew Clive. But that the others knew Clive not all of them knew and only woke up to the fact when they had settled in their seats and started looking round. So while most memorial services take place in an atmosphere of suppressed recognition and reunion to this one was added an element of surprise, many of those present having come along on the assumption they would be among a select few.

Finding this was far from the case the surprise was not untinged with irritation. Or as a go-for-the-throat Australian wordsmith put it to her companion, 'Why, the two-faced pisshole.'

Diffidence was much to the fore. A leading international architect, one of whose airports had recently sprung a leak, came down the centre aisle, and waited at the end of a pew until someone made room, his self-effacing behaviour and downcast eyes proclaiming him a person of some consequence humbled by the circumstances in which he currently found himself and which might have been allegorically represented on a ceiling, say (although not one of his), as Fame deferring to Mortality. 'Do not recognise me,' his look said. 'I am here only to grieve.'

Actually, compared with the soap-stars he hardly counted as famous at all. The world of celebrity in England, at any rate, is small. Whereas fame in America vaults over the barriers of class and profession, lawyers rubbing shoulders with musicians, politicians and stars of stage and screen, in England, television apart, celebrity comes in compartments, *Who's Who* not always the best guide to who's who. Thus here Fame did not always recognise Reputation or Beauty Merit.

A high official in the Treasury, for instance, had got himself seated next to a woman who kept consulting her powder compact, her renown as bubbling game-show host as wasted on him as his skill in succinct summation was lost on her. Worlds collided but with no impact at all, so while what few lawyers there were knew the politicians and some of the civil servants none of them knew the genial wag who pounced on reluctant volunteers and teased out their less than shamefaced confessions on late-night TV. The small-screen gardeners knew the big-screen heart-throbs but none of them recognised 'someone high up in the Bank of England' ('and I don't mean the window-cleaner,' whispered a man who did).

Much noticed, though, was a pop singer who had been known to wear a frock but was today dressed in a suit of stunning sobriety, relieved only by a diamond clasp that had once belonged to Catherine the Great and which was accompanied by an obligatory security guard insisted on by the insurance company. This bovine young man lounged in the pew picking his fingers, happy already to have pinpointed Suspect No. 1, the Waynflete Professor of Moral Philosophy in the University of Oxford who, timid though he was, clearly had villain written all over him.

In front of the Professor was a member of the Government, who was startled to find himself opposite his Permanent Secretary, seated on the other side of the aisle.

'I didn't know you knew Dunlop,' the minister said the next day as they plodded through some meeting on carbon monoxide emissions.

'Oh, I knew him from way back,' said the civil servant airily.

'Me too,' said the minister. 'Way back.'

Actually the minister had only met Clive quite recently, just after he became a minister in fact, but this 'way back' in which both of them took refuge was a time so remote and unspecific that anything that might have happened then was implicitly excused by their youth and the temper of the times. 'I knew him in the Sixties' would have been the same, except that Clive was too young for that.

'At some point,' murmured the minister, 'I want you to take me on one side and explain to me the difference between carbon monoxide and carbon dioxide. Fairly star-studded, wasn't it?'

It was, indeed, a remarkable assembly with philanthropy, scholarship and genuine distinction represented alongside much that was tawdry and merely fashionable, so that with only a little licence this stellar, but tarnished throng might, for all its shortcomings, be taken as a version of England.

And 'a very English occasion' was how it was described by the reporter in the *Telegraph* the next day. Not that she was in a position to know as she hadn't bothered to stay for the service. Currently taking down the names of the last few stragglers she compiled her list, procured a programme of the proceedings, then went off to the

Design Museum to lunch with a colleague.

'After all,' she said over oeufs en gelée, 'they're all the same these occasions. Like sad cocktail parties without the drinks.'

This one as it turned out wasn't, so she got the sack. But it was a nice lunch.

Also thinking how English these occasions tended to be was the young priest in charge, Father Geoffrey Jolliffe. Father Jolliffe was Anglican but with Romish inclinations that were not so much doctrinal as ceremonial and certainly sartorial. Amiable, gregarious and plump, he looked well in the cloak he generally went about in, a priest with a bit of a swish to him. His first curacy had been in a slum parish where, as he put it, 'They like a bit of that,' and since he did too, his ministry got off to a good start and that he chose to call the Eucharist 'Mass' and himself 'Father' troubled no one. His present parish, St Andrew Upchance on the borders of Shoreditch and the City, was also poor, but he had done a good deal to 'turn it round', an achievement that had not gone unnoticed in the diocese, where he was spoken of as a coming man.

There were, it is true, some of his fellow clergy who found him altogether too much, but as he said himself, 'There's not enough of "too much" these days,' and since he was a lively preacher and old-fashioned when it came to the prayer book, a large and loyal congregation seemed to bear this out.

Accustomed at his normal services to women predominating, today Father Jolliffe was not altogether surprised to find so many men turning up. Some of them had been close to Clive, obviously, but that apart, in his experience men needed less cajoling to attend funerals and memorial services than they did normal church (or even the theatre, say) and since men seldom do what they don't want, it had made him wonder why. He decided that where the dead were involved there was always an element of condescension: the deceased had been put in his or her place, namely the grave, and however lavish the tributes with which this was accompanied there was no altering the fact that the situation of the living was altogether superior and to men, in particular, that seemed to appeal.

USUALLY CHEERFUL and expansive, today Father Jolliffe was preoccupied. He had known Clive himself, which accounted for his church being the somewhat out of the way venue for the memorial service. His death had come as an unpleasant surprise, as, like so many in the congregation, he had not known Clive was even ill. It was sad, too, of course, 'a shared sadness' as he planned to say, but for him, as for others in the congregation, it was somewhat worrying also (though he had no plans to say that).

Still, if he was anxious he did not intend to let it affect his performance. 'And,' as he had recently insisted to a Diocesan Selection Board, 'a service is a performance. Devout, sincere and given wholeheartedly for God, but a performance nevertheless.'

The Board, on the whole, had been impressed.

By coincidence the subject of memorial services had come up at the Board when Father Jolliffe, suppressing a fastidious shudder, had heard himself describe such occasions as 'a challenge'. Urged to expand he had shared his vision of the church packed with unaccustomed worshippers come together, as they thought, simply to commemorate a loved one but also (though they might not know it) hungering for that hope and reassurance which it was the clergy's job to satisfy. This, too, had gone down well with the Board though most them, Father Jolliffe included, knew it was tosh.

The truth was memorial services were a bugger. For all its shortcomings in the way of numbers a regular congregation was in church because it wanted to be or at least felt it ought to be. It's true that looking down from the pulpit on his flock Sunday by Sunday Father Jolliffe sometimes felt that God was not much more than a pastime; that these were churchgoers as some people were pigeon-fanciers or collectors of stamps, gentle, mildly eccentric and hanging onto the end of something. Still, on a scale ranging from fervent piety to mere respectability these regular worshippers were at least like-minded: they had come together to worship God and even with their varying degrees of certainty that there was a God to worship the awkward question of belief seldom arose.

With a memorial service, and a smart one at

that, God was an embarrassment and Father Jolliffe was reminded of this when he had his first sight of the congregation. He had left his service book in his stall and nipping across to get it before putting on his robes he was taken aback at the packed and murmuring pews. Few of those attending, he suspected, had on taking their seats bowed their heads in prayer or knew that that was (once anyway) the form. Few would know the hymns, and still fewer the prayers. Yet he was shortly going to have to stand up and ask them to collaborate in the fiction that they all believed in God (or something anyway) and even that there was an after-life. So what he had said to the Board had been right. It was a challenge, the challenge being that most of them would think this an insult to their intelligence.

How Father Jolliffe was going to cope with this dilemma was interesting Treacher. Indeed it was partly what had brought him to St Andrew's on this particular morning. There were various ways round it, the best of which, in Treacher's view, was not to get round it at all; ignore it in fact, a priest retaining more respect if he led the congregation in prayer with neither explanation nor apology, the assumption being that they were all believers and if not, since they were in the house of God, it behoved them to pretend to be so. Taking the uncompromising line, though, meant that it was hard then for the clergyman to get on those friendly, informal terms with the congregation that such an occasion seemed to require. Treacher did not see this as a drawback. A priest himself, although in mufti, getting on friendly terms with the congregation had never been high on his list.

Father Jolliffe would not have agreed. 'Whatever else it is,' he had told the Board, 'a congregation is first and foremost an audience. And I am the stand-up. I must win them over.' It was another bold-seeming sentiment that had hit the spot, occasioning some laughter, it's true, but also much sage nodding, though not, Father Jolliffe had noticed, from Canon Treacher, who was an archdeacon and not enthusiastic about congregations in the first place. Treacher (and his fiercely sharpened pencil) was the only one of the Board who had made him nervous (the Bishop was a sweetie), so it was a blessing that on this particular morning, thanks to Canon Treacher's precautions, the priest remained unaware of his presence.

The worst tack a priest could adopt at a service such as this, and a trap Treacher was pretty confident Father Jolliffe was going to fall into, was to acknowledge at the start that the congregation (or 'friends' as Treacher had even heard them called) might not subscribe to the beliefs implicit in the hymns and prayers but that they should on no account feel badly about this but instead substitute appropriate sentiments of their own. ('I believe this stuff but you don't have to.') Since in Treacher's experience there would be few in the church with appropriate sentiments still less beliefs to hand, this meant that if the congregation thought of anything at all during the prayers (which he doubted) it was just to try and summon up a picture of the departed sufficient to squeeze out the occasional tear.

Treacher, it has to be said, had some reason for his pessimism. Casting an eye over the Order of Service Treacher noted that in addition to a saxophone solo a fashionable baritone from

Covent Garden was down to sing 'Some Enchanted Evening'. With such delights in prospect Canon Treacher feared that liturgical rigour would not be high on the list.

What approach he was going to take to the service ('what angle the priest should come at it') Father Jolliffe had not yet decided, though since he was even now being robed in the vestry it might be thought there was not much time. But he had never been methodical, his sermon often no more than a few headings or injunctions to himself on the back of the parish notes: though on this occasion he had not even bothered with that, preferring, as he would have said, to 'wing it'. This was less slipshod than it sounded, as he genuinely believed that in this 'winging' there was an element of the divine. He had never thought it out but felt that the wings were God-sent, an angel's possibly, or another version of 'Thy wings' under the shadow of which he bade the faithful hide Sunday by Sunday.

He slipped out of the vestry and made his way round the outside of the church to join the choir now assembled at the West door. When he had been appointed vicar at St Andrew's processions generally began obscurely at the vestry winding their awkward way round past the pulpit and up the chancel steps. Father Jolliffe felt that this was untheatrical and missing a trick so one of his first innovations was to make the entrance of the choir and clergy bolder and more dramatic, routeing the procession down the centre of the church.

The procession should have been headed and the choir preceded by a crucifer bearing the processional cross (another innovation), but since this was a weekday Leo, the crucifer, had not been able to get time off work. A beefy young man, Leo was a bus driver and Father Jolliffe had always taken quiet pride in that fact and would occasionally cite him at diocesan conferences as a modern update of the calling of the disciples ('Matthew may have been a tax-collector. What's so special about that? Our crucifer happens to be a bus driver'). Though Leo would much have preferred marching down the centre aisle to where he currently was, stuck behind the wheel of a No. 74 inching up Putney High Street, since privatisation religious obligation was no longer accepted as a reason for absence. 'Or believe me, my son,' said the supervisor, 'come Ramadan and our Sikh and Hindu brethren who compose a substantial proportion of the workforce would be up at the mosque when we need them down at the depot. I'm not without religious feeling myself and my sister-in-law was nearly a nun but sorry, no can do.'

Still, what the procession lacked in splendour at the front it made up in dignity at the back, as in addition to Father Jolliffe also attending the service were several other clergymen, one of them indeed a suffragan bishop. None of them was personally known to Father Jolliffe or seemingly to each other, but all were presumably known to Clive. Though got up in all their gear they were not attending in any official capacity (and in the *Telegraph* report of the occasion they would be described as 'robed and in the sanctuary'), but they definitely brought a kick to the rear of the column which was now assembled and waiting to begin its journey towards the chancel.

The organist was meanwhile playing an arrangement of Samuel Barber's Adagio for

Strings which many in the congregation were enjoying, having been made familiar with the tune from its frequent airings on Classic FM. Seeing no conclusion in the offing Father Jolliffe pressed a button behind a pillar to alert the organist that they were ready to begin. The Barber now came to a sharp and unceremonious close but since random terminations were not unusual on Classic FM, nobody noticed.

Now from somewhere at the back of the church Father Jolliffe's voice rang out, 'Would you stand' and the church shuffled to its feet. 'We shall sing the first hymn on your Order of Service, "Love Divine All Loves Excelling".'

Once upon a time it would have been enough to announce the hymn and the congregation would have known to stand. Hymns you stand, prayers you kneel. Nowadays it was prayers you sit, hymns you wait and see what other people are going to do. 'Love,' Father Jolliffe reproached himself. 'We must love one another.'

Now the clergy began to follow the choir down the aisle, Father Jolliffe bringing up the rear, singing the hymn without consulting the words, long since off the book and thus free while singing heartily to cast professionally loving glances to right and left, on his pink and generous face an expression of settled benevolence.

He had still not decided how to pitch his opening remarks, trusting even now that something would occur, in some ways the closest he got to faith in God this trust that when it came to the point words would be put into his mouth. As he passed through the worshippers raggedly singing the hymn, Father Jolliffe thought they looked less like a congregation than an audience, smart, worldly and doubtless expecting him to keep God very much on the back burner. He resented this a little, because, though he was a sophisticated priest and too self-forgiving, his faith was real enough, though so supple and riddled with irony that God was no more exempt from censure than the Archbishop of Canterbury (whom he privately referred to as Old Potato-Face). Still, he resented having to tailor his beliefs to his audience and not for the first time wished he was an out and out Catholic where this problem wouldn't arise. One of the many grumbles Father Jolliffe had about the

English Reformation was that it was then that feeling had got into the service, so you couldn't get away with just saying the words but had to mean them at the same time.

These thoughts had taken him and the procession to the chancel, where the choir filed into their pews and the spare clergy disposed themselves around, while still leaving the hymn with a couple of verses to run. This gave Father Jolliffe a chance to think about what he ought to say about Clive and what he ought not to say.

CLIVE had been a masseur; there was no secret about that. It was something he was very good at and his skill transcended mere physical manipulation. Many of his clients attested to a feeling of warmth that seemed to flow through his fingers and for which there was no orthodox physiological explanation. 'He has healing hands' was one way of putting it or (this from the more mystically inclined) 'He has the Touch.'

That Clive was black (though palely so) was thought by some to account for these healing attributes since it meant (despite his having been born and brought up in Bethnal Green) that he was closer to his origins than were his clients and in touch with an ancient wisdom long since lost to them. Never discouraging these mythic speculations Clive himself had no such illusions, though the pouch to which he sometimes stripped to carry out the massage was rudimentary enough to call up all sorts of primitive musings.

The heat that his clients felt, though, was not fanciful and as a boy had embarrassed Clive and made him reluctant to touch or be touched. The realisation that what he had was not a burden but a gift was a turning point and that, with his calorific propensities, it could be marketed was another. And so the laying on of hands became for him a way of life.

This was not, of course, all. Though Clive was scrupulous never to omit the ceremony of massage, for some it was just the preliminary to a more protracted and intimate encounter and one which might, understandably, come a little dearer. Looking over the crowded church, Father Jolliffe wondered who were here just as grateful patients whose burden of pain Clive had smoothed away and who had come along to commemorate the easing of a different sort of burden, and of the latter how many were as nervous as he was himself about the legacy that the dead man might have left them.

Now as the hymn ended Father Jolliffe said, 'Will you sit', gave them a moment to settle and then launched into his preamble. And straightaway came out with something he had no intention of saying.

'On such occasions as these,' he said, 'a priest will often preface his remarks with an apology, craving the forgiveness of the congregation since they have had the advantage of knowing the deceased whereas he didn't. I make no such apology. I knew Clive and like most of you, I imagine, loved him and valued his friendship – else why are any of us here?'

Treacher, who was not here for that at all, made a neat note on the back of his Order of Service.

Father Jolliffe was amazed at himself. Few people in the congregation were aware he knew Clive and for various reasons, one of which was prudence, he hadn't been planning to say that he did. Now he had blurted it out and must make the best of it, though this would be hard as there was so much he could not say.

For the most part Geoffrey (and there are some circumstances in which it's right he is called Geoffrey and not Father Jolliffe) . . . for the most part Geoffrey was celibate, though he attached no virtue to this, knowing it was not abstinence so much as lack of opportunity that kept him generally unconjugate; that and a certain timidity where sex was concerned which made him, despite his (mild) moral disapproval, bestow on an enterprising promiscuity such as Clive's an almost heroic status. No matter that boldness came as naturally to Clive as diffidence did to Geoffrey or that Clive, of course, was much better looking and unburdened by Geoffrey's thoughts of God (and not looking a fool); Geoffrey knew that in what nowadays is called a one-to-one situation he was what he thought of as shy, so that men who weren't shy, such as Clive, seemed to him warriors, their valour, however profligate, more of a virtue than his own timorous drawing back.

Geoffrey had had experience at first hand of how fly Clive could be. En route for lunch together along the Farringdon Road (not a thoroughfare Geoffrey had ever thought of in a carnal context) Clive had intercepted a male glance that Geoffrey had not even noticed and quick as a fish he had darted away leaving Geoffrey to eat alone and return home disconsolate, where Clive duly came by to give an account of his afternoon. True, Clive was not choosy or how else would he have got into bed with Geoffrey himself, episodes so decorous that for Clive they can scarcely have registered as sex at all, though still tactile enough for Geoffrey, on the news of Clive's death, to be filled with unease.

Being of an Anglo-Catholic persuasion Father Jolliffe practised auricular confession, when he would come clean about his predilections, an ordeal that was somewhat diminished by choosing as his confessor a clergyman whom he knew 'had no problem with that' and being of a similar persuasion himself would place it low down in the hierarchy of possible wickedness. With never much to confess on that particular score, now with Clive gone there was going to be even less.

Somebody coughed. The congregation were waiting and though the pause while Father Jolliffe wrestled with what he should and should not say was understood to be one of deep personal remembrance or even a chance to regain control of his feelings, still, there wasn't all day.

Father Jolliffe plunged on and suddenly it all came right. 'We shall be singing some hymns. We shall pray together and there will be readings and some of Clive's favourite music.' Father Jolliffe paused. 'Prayer may seem to some of you an outmoded activity and hymns too, possibly, but that was not what Clive thought. Clive, as I know personally, was always keen to involve himself in the rites and rituals of the church and were he here he would be singing louder and praying harder than anybody.'

Despite the unintentional disclosure of his friendship with Clive, Father Jolliffe was not displeased with how he (or possibly God) had turned it to good account. Using Clive as a way round any misgivings the congregation might have re the religious side of things was a happy thought. It took the curse off the service very nicely and in the shadows behind the pillar Treacher made another note and this time added a tick.

Actually Geoffrey (we are back to Geoffrey again) knew that where Clive's religious inclinations were concerned he was stretching it a bit. Pious he wasn't and his interest in the rites and rituals of the church didn't go much further than the not unfetching young men who were often helping to perform them, Clive reckoning, not always correctly, that what with the ceremony, the incense and the general dressing-up anyone of a religious disposition was, as he put it, 'halfway there already'. He was particularly keen on vestments, though not in any way Father Jolliffe (sorry) could share with the congregation, having once found Clive in the rectory clad only in his underpants trying on cotta and cope.

Father Jolliffe now led the congregation in prayer, asking them to kneel if they so chose or simply bow their heads so that they could together remember Clive. Heads went down, eyes were closed with only the security guard on the qui vive, scowling across the bowed benches where someone, he felt sure, might be only pretending to pray. At one point he even stood up and turned round lest some wrongdoer could be taking advantage of these unstructured devotions in order to creep up and snatch the clasp. Suspicious, as he put it, 'of this whole prayer thing' he slumped back moodily in his seat as Jolliffe launched into the Collect.

The vicar didn't improvise prayers, Treacher was relieved to note, drawing them from the ample stock of the old prayer book, and saying them briskly and formally as Treacher preferred them to be said. There were few things worse, in Treacher's view, than a priest who gave too much weight to the words of prayers, pausing as if to invest them with heartfelt meaning and thereby impressing the congregation (and himself) with his sincerity. Treacher had even heard the Lord's Prayer delivered in this fashion and found it intolerable and even queasy. But Father Jolliffe, perhaps because of his Catholic leanings, was dry and to the point. 'Say the word, say the word only' seemed to be his motto and Treacher added another tick.

So far, Treacher was bound to admit, Jolliffe was not doing too badly. Even the news of the priest's friendship with the dead man had scarcely counted against him, as the Archdeacon had all along assumed Jolliffe to be homosexual, though without seeing this as a cause for censure or even a necessary obstacle to promotion. Untrammelled by wife or family and with a housekeeper to look after the vicarage (when there were still vicarages to look after), their energies channelled, the sex under wraps, once upon a time homosexuals had made excellent priests and still could so long as they were sensible. The homosexuals Treacher preferred were dry, acerbic and, of course, unavowed; A.E. Housman the type that he approved of, minus the poetry, of course, and (though this was less important) minus the atheism. Nowadays, though, discretion had been cast aside and it had all gone splashy, priests feeling in conscience bound to make their proclivities plain, with even Jolliffe's declaration of friendship for the dead man a timorous attempt, Treacher felt, to lay his cards on the table. Which was a mistake, Treacher believing that a priest should no more declare a sexual preference than he should a political one. Even so, Treacher reflected, there was this to be said in Jolliffe's favour that, whatever his shortcomings, he was not she. In Treacher's church there was a place for she, running the jumble sale, or doing the altar flowers; a she could even take the plate round or read the lesson. But there was no place for she at the altar or in the pulpit. So, give Jolliffe his due: he was not she.

Now the congregation sat and the scheduled part of the service began. The programme had been put together by Pam, a cheerful woman Clive had known since childhood and who was now a producer at the BBC, and Derek, his long-time landlord. Eclectic would be the kindest word to describe it. Treacher, who had no reason to be kind, thought it looked a bit of a ragbag.

First up was a well-known actress and star of a current sitcom who ascends the stairs of the lectern where she reads immaculately a piece about death not really being the end but just like popping next door. It was a regular standard at memorial services and seeing it billed in the programme Treacher had sighed. He believed in death and when he said he believed in God, death was to a large extent what he meant. These days people didn't, or tried not to, always feeling death was unfair, so when they saw it coming to them or their loved ones they made a great song and dance about it.

And these days there was always blame; it was 'down to' someone or other – the school, the doctor, the police – and you must fight back, that was today's philosophy; in the midst of life we are in death was nowadays a counsel for wimps. It didn't used to be like this, he thought. Had it come from America, he wondered. Or Liverpool? Was television to blame? Or Mrs Thatcher? These days he seldom felt well himself but he wasn't complaining. Or perhaps (and here he was trying to be charitable) what was really distasteful was death as leveller. These days people were so anxious to lay hold of anything that marked them out from the rest – the death of their children, for instance, their neglect by hospitals, being fumbled when young or tortured by nuns; even the murder of loved ones would do if it served to single them out. Whereas the good thing about death was that it singled everybody out. It was the one unchanging thing.

Treacher smiled.

Father Jolliffe's thoughts were different, though just as wayward and far from Clive. The next reader had a ponytail and Geoffrey found himself wondering at what point in bed the hair was unloosed, shaken out, let down. And by whom? He thought of the curtain of hair falling across the pillow, the signal, perhaps (in addition to other signals), that the body was now on offer. So again he remembered Clive.

Next up was a pianist, another personal acquaintance who comes to the piano in mittens which he then takes off before playing some Schubert, the performance of which, judging by his expression, seems to cause him exquisite pain but which turns to dark-faced anger as during the final section a police car drives past with its siren going.

And so it goes on, under Father Jolliffe's benevolent eye, poems, readings, a succession of 'turns' really, one of which, though, Treacher is pleased to note, is from St Paul's First Letter to the Corinthians, the passage about love, with Father Jolliffe opting for the King James version using charity. He took time at the start of the reading to explain to the congregation that charity was love and not anything to do with flag days or people in doorways. Or if it was to do with people in doorways that was only one of its meanings.

Treacher would have scorned such condescension and let the congregation make of it what they could but he forbore to mark his card on the point. Still, he would have preferred it if the great rolling cadences of the Authorised Version hadn't been followed by a saxophone rendition of the Dusty Springfield standard, 'You don't have to say you love me', a number (and there was no other word for it) that occasioned a round of applause, from which Treacher unsurprisingly abstained.

During the saxophone solo Geoffrey's worries about Clive recurred. What had he died of? He wished he knew for certain. Or not. Geoffrey had been in bed with Clive seldom and so tamely that only someone as inexperienced as Geoffrey would have thought himself at risk at all. But it did happen, he knew that; he wasn't even sure if there was some risk in kissing (though there hadn't been much of that either).

The truth was it was God that Geoffrey didn't trust. Irony was always the deity's strong point and to afflict a transgressor as timid as Geoffrey with such a disproportionate penalty might appeal to the Almighty's sense of cosmic fun. It was unfair to God, he knew, but he'd always felt the deity had a mean side and on one of his reports at theological college his tutor had written, 'Tends to confuse God with Joan Crawford.'

Treacher looked at his watch. One or two of the participants had preceded their contributions with a few words about Clive – Clive as assiduous and imaginative hospital visitor, Clive as holiday companion, Clive as lover of Schubert and dogs. Still, though these had lengthened the proceedings a little, Treacher was relieved to note that they were now on the last item before the final hymn, a rendering by an ancient musical comedy actress of 'darling Ivor's' immortal 'Fly home, little heart'. 'Fly home, Clive,' she prefaced it, 'our thoughts go with you.'

As her quavering soprano drifted through the church, Treacher began to make plans to slip away as unobtrusively as he had arrived. Slightly to the Archdeacon's regret he had to concede that Father Jolliffe had not done too badly. He had kept the service moving and each contribution brief: he had not sold God short and even allowing for the saxophone solo and the old lady currently in full, if tiny, voice it had never ceased to be a church service. Treacher had come along hoping to find Father Jolliffe a bit of a clown and over-anxious to please. There had been no evidence of that and he deserved credit. Canon Treacher folded his Order of Service and put it in his pocket. He would nip out during the last hymn.

FATHER JOLLIFFE, too, was pleased the service was over in such good time, though he had some regrets. Varied though the contributions had been he didn't feel they had done justice to Clive and his special charm. Nobody had quite captured his character; an opportunity had been missed. Besides, Father Jolliffe (and he can surely be forgiven) was still somewhat star-struck by his glamorous congregation and understandably wanted to hold onto them for just a little longer. They were such a change from his usual attendance who (while just as precious

48

in the sight of God, of course) were duller and less fun.

So when the old lady finished and was greeted with such sympathetic applause she had to be coaxed from the microphone before she got into an encore, Father Jolliffe on a sudden impulse (with which he subsequently thought God had had something to do) didn't sink to his knees for the final prayers but stood up, moved to the centre of the chancel steps and expressed the hope that anyone with cherished memories of Clive which they would like to share should now feel free to do so. Treacher frowned and fished the Order of Service out of his pocket to check that this was a departure from the published proceedings. Finding that it was and the proceedings had indeed been prolonged he put a large question-mark in the margin.

Father Jolliffe stood on the chancel steps and in the expectant silence the ponderous workings of the clock, fixed on the back wall of the tower, now began to click and whirr preparatory to slowly striking 12. From experience Father Jolliffe knew that these crankings made speech impossible, so hearing those first admonitory

49

clicks he had learned to pause and wait until the ancient mechanism had run its course.

These necessary cessations often had an opportuneness to them, coming at a pause in a prayer, say, or, as today, at a moment of remembrance, just as year by year the coughing and wheezing ushered in the start of the grandest remembrance of all, the Two-Minute Silence. The unorchestrated pauses, though, were generally less weighty than that but were so repeatedly apposite as to have acquired an almost liturgical significance, the whirring of the cogs and the clanking of the wheels serving to charge the moment, as did the ringing of the bell at the elevation of the Host.

In matters of faith Father Jolliffe might be thought a bit of a noodle but however felicitous the pause in question even he didn't quite identify it as the voice of God. Still, if it was not God speaking, sometimes he felt the Almighty was at least clearing his throat, coughing meaningfully as a reminder of his presence. Father Jolliffe could see no harm in the practice of the presence of God being conflated with the sound of the passage of time, though there were also occasions when the clock's timely intervention irritated him, feeling that there was no need sometimes for the deity to draw attention to himself so obviously. It had something of St Peter and the cock crowing thrice about it, not an incident Father Jolliffe was particularly fond of as it showed Jesus up as a bit of an 'I told you so', which on the quiet the priest felt he sometimes was anyway.

Today, though, the intervention of the clock was useful in that it gave the congregation a moment or two to dwell on what they might want to say about Clive and perhaps as a consequence once 12 had struck people were not slow to respond.

A man was straightaway on his feet testifying to Clive's skill and good humour crewing in a transatlantic yacht race and another to his unsuspected abilities as a gourmet cook, testimonials greeted with incredulity in some sections of the congregation ('Clive?') but elsewhere without surprise. A woman said what a good gardener he was and how he had gone on to paint her kitchen, while someone from Woman's Hour described him as 'bright-eyed and bushy-tailed' and evidenced the large congregation as a testimony to Clive's genius for friendship, a genius incidentally that is generally posthumous and, like 'touching life at many points' (which Clive was also said to have done), is only found in obituaries. On the other hand, 'not suffering fools gladly', another staple of the obituary column, was not said, Clive having suffered fools as a matter of course as this was partly what he was paid for.

A Japanese gentleman now stood up and addressed the congregation in Japanese, a series of emphatic and seemingly impassioned declarations of which no one, even those lucky enough to speak Japanese, understood a word, as the acoustics of the church (designed by Inigo Jones) made it sound like overhearing an argument. Still, whether out of admiration for his boldness in speaking at all or to compensate him for being Japanese and therefore unintelligible, the congregation gave him a round of applause.

He bowed to every corner of the church then sat down, by which time there were already two more people on their feet wanting to have a word. Treacher began to think his estimate of Father Jolliffe to have been wrong. There was no firm hand here and as a woman behind him said, 'It's going on a bit,' the Archdeacon made another adverse note.

Happy to see it go on was a publisher, a portly and pretentious figure who had never met Clive but was there escorting one of his authors (as yet unennobled), a woman with several bestsellers under her belt but whose work had recently taken a feminist turn and who he feared might be looking for a publisher to match. Coming along to the service just as a chore he had been amazed at the level and variety of celebrity represented and, in the way of publishers, began to scent a book. As more and more of the congregation stood up and the reminiscences about Clive accumulated the publisher grew steadily more excited, occasionally clutching his companion's arm or, like Treacher (but not), scribbling notes on the back of his Order of Service. He saw the book as quick and easy to produce, a tape-recording job largely, a collage of interviews each no more than two or three paragraphs long – a book for people who preferred newspapers and which read like gossip while masquerading as sociology. 'A portrait of a generation'.

Her affection for Clive notwithstanding the novelist found it hard to reciprocate the publisher's enthusiasm, her own work never having generated a comparable degree of fervour. A woman would understand. As the publisher jotted down the names of possible writers she determined to take her next book where it would be better appreciated. She yawned.

Others were yawning too. Now an elderly couple got up and left, followed a few minutes later by a younger man, tapping his watch, portraying helplessness and mouthing 'Sorry' to an unidentified friend in one of the pews behind.

FATHER JOLLIFFE was now wishing he'd never let the congregation off the leash. They were popping up all over the place, never fewer than two people on their feet waiting their turn. Some didn't stand but put a hand up, one of the most persistent a drab youth in an anorak sitting towards the front on the aisle. How he had come to know Clive Father Jolliffe could not imagine.

As a woman ended some protracted hymn to Clive's 'nurturing touch' Father Jolliffe managed to get in before the next speaker. 'I feel,' he said tentatively, 'that as time's getting on we ought to think about drawing these delightful reminiscences to a close,' a warning word that had the opposite effect to that intended as it galvanised all those who had not yet made up their minds to speak now to try and do so. In particular it made the drab youth start waving his hand as if he were still at school and trying to catch the teacher's eye. He looked as if he was at school, too, in jeans and blue anorak, though he had made some effort to dress up for the occasion by putting on a shirt and tie, the shirt rather too big at the collar and the cuffs almost covering his hands. Father Jolliffe wished he would be more forthright and not wait to be called but just stand up and get on with it like other people were doing, currently a philosopher, well-groomed and bronzed from a sabbatical at Berkeley.

'Though we knew his name was Clive,' he was

saying, 'we' – his wife sitting beside him smiled – 'we called him Max, a name I came to feel suited him well. It's not entirely a nice name, not plain certainly or wholesome. In fact Max, really, is the name of a charmer, implying a degree of sophistication, a veneer of social accomplishment. It's urban, metropolitan, the name of someone who could take a vacant place at a poker game, say, and raise no eyebrows, which someone called . . . oh, Philip, say, couldn't.'

At this a woman in front turned round. 'I called him Philip.' Then turning to her neighbour. 'He said that was what he felt like inside.'

'I called him Bunny,' said a man on the aisle and this was the signal for other names to be tossed around – Toby, Alex and even Denis, all, however unlikely, attested to and personally guaranteed by various members of the congregation – so that still on his feet to bear witness to the unique appropriateness of Max the philosopher begins to feel a bit of a fool and says lamely, 'Well, he was always Max to us but this was obviously a many-sided man ... which is yet another cause for celebration.' And sits down plumply to a reassuring pat from his wife.

One of the names submitted in contention with Max was Betty, the claims for which had been quite belligerently advanced by a smallish young man in a black suit and shaven head who was sitting towards the front with several other young men similarly suited and shorn, one or two of them with sunglasses lodged on top of their hairless heads.

Now, ignoring the woman whose turn it was and the feebly waving youth, the young man, who gave his name as Carl, addressed the congregation. 'Knowing Clive well I think he would be touched if someone' – he meant himself – 'were to say something about him as a lover?'

A couple who had just got up to go straightaway sat down again. There was a hush, then a woman in the front row said: 'Excuse me. Before you do that I think we ought to see if this lady minds.' She indicated her neighbour, a shabby old woman in a battered straw hat, her place also occupied by a couple of greasy shopping bags. 'She might mind. She is Mr Dunlop's aunt.'

Father Jolliffe closed his eyes in despair. It was Miss Wishart and she was not Clive's aunt at all. Well into her eighties and with nothing better to do Miss Wishart came to every funeral or memorial service that took place at the church, which was at least warm and where she could claim to be a distant relative of the deceased, a pretence not hard to maintain as she was genuinely hard of hearing and so could ignore the occasional probing question. Sometimes when she was lucky (and the relatives were stupid) she even got invited back for the funeral tea. All this Father Jolliffe knew and could have said, but it was already too late as Carl was even now sauntering round to the front pew where Miss Wishart was sitting in order to put the question to her directly.

With set face and making no concessions to her age or sensibilities Carl stood over Miss Wishart. 'Do you mind if we talk about your nephew's sex life?' Her neighbour repeated this in Miss Wishart's ear and while she considered the question, which she heard as having to do with his ex-wife, Carl looked up at Father Jolliffe. 'And you don't object, padre?'

It's often hard these days for the clergy not to think of God as a little old-fashioned and Father Jolliffe was no exception. So if he was going to object it wasn't on grounds of taste or decorum but simply in order to cut the service short. But what he really objected to was the condescension of 'padre' (and even its hint of a sneer) so this made him feel he couldn't object on any grounds at all without the young man thinking he was a ninny.

'No, I've no objection,' he said, 'except' – and he looked boldly down at this small-headed creature – 'I think what we're talking about is love. Clive's love life.' Then, thinking that didn't sound right either, 'His life of love.'

That sounded even worse and the young man smirked.

Treacher sighed. Jolliffe had been given an opportunity to put a stop to all this nonsense and he had muffed it. Had he been in charge he would have put the young man in his place, got the congregation on their knees and the service would have been over in five minutes. Now there was no telling what would happen.

As an indication that the proceedings were descending into chaos Treacher noted that one or two men in the congregation now felt relaxed enough to take out mobile phones and carry on hushed conversations, presumably rearranging appointments for which the length of the service was now making them late. The young man in front pocketed his cigarettes and lighter and strolled up the aisle to slip out of the West door where he found that two or three other like-minded smokers had preceded him. They nattered moodily in nicotine's enforced camaraderie before grinding their fags into the gravestones and rejoining the service at the point where the question about her nephew's sex life had at last got through to Miss Wishart and her neighbour was able to announce the verdict to the congregation. 'His aunt doesn't mind.'

There was a smattering of applause to signify approval of such exemplary open-mindedness in one so old, but since the question Miss Wishart thought she'd been asked was not to do with her nephew's sex life but with his next life, her tolerance hadn't really been put to the test.

'I JUST THOUGHT,' said Carl standing on the chancel steps, 'that it would be kind of nice to say what Clive was like in bed?' It was a question but not one that expected an answer. 'I mean, not in detail, obviously, only that he was good? He took his time and without being, you know, mechanical he was really inventive? I want,' he said, 'to take you on a journey? A journey round Clive's body?'

Treacher sank lower in his seat and Geoffrey's smile lost some of its benevolence as Carl did just that, dwelling on each part, genitals for the moment excepted, with the fervour if not quite the language of the metaphysical poets.

Though it was a body Geoffrey was at least acquainted with, Carl's version of it rang no bells and so he was reassured when he saw one or two in the congregation smiling wistfully and shaking their heads as if Carl had missed the point of Clive's body. Still, Geoffrey hoped nobody was going to feel strongly enough about this discrepancy to offer up a rival version as, however fascinating this material was, he felt there was a limit to what the congregation would stand.

'Do we really want to know this?' a senior official in the Foreign Office muttered to his wife (though in truth he knew some of it already and unbeknownst to him, so did she).

Actually Geoffrey was surprised at Carl's forbearance in omitting the penis, an intimate survey of which he was obviously capable of providing did he so choose. Perhaps, Geoffrey thought, he was saving it up but if so it was to no purpose as it was while Carl was en route from the scrotum to the anus that suddenly it all got too much and a man was bold enough to shout out: 'Shame.'

Carl rounded on him fiercely. 'No, there was no shame. No shame then and no shame now. If you didn't understand that about Clive, you shouldn't be here.'

After which, though there were no more interruptions, the congregation felt slightly bullied and so took on a mildly mutinous air.

A woman sitting near to the front and quite close to Carl said almost conversationally: 'And you made this journey quite often, did you?'

'What journey?'

'Round Clive's body.'

'Sure. Why?'

'It's just that, while I may be making a fool of myself here,' and she looked round for support, 'I didn't know he was . . . that way.'

Several women who were within earshot nodded agreement.

'To me he was – ' and she knew she was on dangerous ground, 'to me, he wasn't that way at all.'

Carl frowned. 'Do you mean gay?'

The woman (she was a buyer for Marks and Spencer's) smiled kindly and nodded.

'Well let me tell you,' said Carl, 'he was "that way".'

Though these exchanges are intimate and conversational they filter back through the congregation where they are greeted with varying degrees of astonishment, some of it audible.

'She didn't know?'

'Who's she kidding?'

'Clive,' the woman went on, 'never gave me to suppose that his sexual preferences were other than normal.'

'It *is* normal,' shouted Carl.

'I apologise. I mean conventional.'

'It's conventional, too.'

'Straight then,' said the buyer with a gesture of defeat. 'Let's say straight.'

'Say what you fucking like,' said Carl, 'only he

wasn't. He was gay.'

Smiling and unconvinced she shook her head but said no more.

During this exchange Geoffrey had been thinking about Carl's hair or lack of it, the gleam of his skull through the blond stubble making him look not unlike a piglet. Once upon a time hair as short as this would have been a badge of a malignant disposition, a warning to keep clear, with long hair indicating a corresponding lenity. With its hint of social intransigence it had become a badge of sexual deviance, which it still seemed to be, though nowadays it was also a useful mask for incipient baldness, cutting the hair short a way of pre-empting the process.

'Fucking' had put a stop to these musings though Carl had said it so casually that for all they were in church no one seemed shocked (Treacher fortunately hadn't heard it) and Father Jolliffe decided to let it pass.

In his fencing match with the buyer from M&S Carl had undoubtedly come out on top but it had plainly disconcerted him and though he resumed his journey round Clive's body, when he got to his well-groomed armpits he decided to call it a day. 'When someone dies so young,' he summed up, 'the pity of it and the waste of it touch us all. But when he or she dies of Aids' – someone in the congregation gave a faint cry – 'there should be anger as well as pity, and a resolve to fight this insidious disease and the prejudice it arouses and not to rest until we have a cure.' Carl sat down to be embraced by two of his friends, his stubbly head rubbed by a third.

HEARING Aids mentioned for the first time and what had hitherto been vague fears and suspicions now given explicit corroboration many in the congregation found it hard to hide their concern, this death which had hitherto been an occasion for sorrow now a cause for alarm.

One woman sobbed openly, comforted by her (slightly pensive) husband.

A man knelt down and prayed, his companion stroking his back gently as he did so.

'I didn't think you needed to die of it any more,' a round the world yachtswoman whispered to her husband. 'I thought there were drugs.'

Others just sat there stunned, their own fate now prefigured, this memorial service a rehearsal for their own.

One of these, of course, was Father Jolliffe who is professional enough, though, to think this sobering down might be given prayerful expression, all this worry and concern channelled into an invocation not only for Clive but for all the victims of this frightful disease and not merely here but in Africa, Asia and America and so on. The landscape of the petition taking shape in his mind he stood up and faced the congregation. 'Shall we pray.'

As he himself knelt he saw the student-type in the anorak, impervious to the atmosphere obviously, still with his hand up and waving it even more vigorously now. But enough had been said and the priest ignored him.

There is a hush, with Treacher relieved that Father Jolliffe has at last got a grip on the service and is now going to bring these unseemly proceedings to a fitting conclusion.

'Vicar.'

It was the young man in the anorak. His voice was very clear in the silence and those of the congregation who had knelt or just put their heads down now raised them to look and Treacher, who had felt this service could hold no more surprises, said 'Oh God' and would have put his head in his hands had it not been there already.

Even the easy-going Father Jolliffe was taken aback at this unheard-of interruption. 'I was praying,' he said reproachfully.

He thought the young man blushed but he was looking so worked up it was hard to tell. A long-wristed, narrow-faced, straight-shouldered young man now looking sheepish. 'I did have my hand up before,' he said. 'And besides, it's probably relevant to the prayer.'

Had it not come at such an inopportune moment the notion that a prayer needed to be up to the minute and take account of all relevant information would have merited some thought and indeed might have provided a useful subject for 'Faith and Time', the series of discussion groups Father Jolliffe was currently running after Evensong on Sundays; the topicality of intercession in the light of the omniscience of God, for instance, or prayers taking place in time and God not. As it was the priest found himself staring at the young man, all pastoral feeling suspended, and saying rather crossly, 'Well?'

'My name is Hopkins,' said the young man. 'I'm on my year out. I'm going to do geology. I was in South America looking at rocks.'

Some of this he said loudly enough for the congregation to hear, but other less relevant remarks he gave almost as an aside to the near-by pews, so that somebody out of range said: 'What?'

'On his year out, doing geology,' somebody else called back.

'And?' said somebody else under their breath.

'I got sponsorship from Tilcon,' the young man added redundantly.

Somebody sighed heavily and said: 'Do we need to know this?'

'That was why I was in Peru. The rocks are very good there.'

'Can't hear,' said a well-known commentator on the arts. 'I know about Peru and even I can't hear.'

A woman nearby smiled kindly at the boy, and

indicated he should speak up.

'The thing is' – and the speaking up made him sound defiant – 'I was staying in the same hotel as Mr Dunlop when he died, and he didn't die of Aids.'

Finding him so unprepossessing and with no air of authority whatever (and, it has to be said, younger than most of their children) the congregation were disinclined to give him much attention. What had seemed just another tedious reminiscence is at first listlessly received and it's only when the glad message 'Not Aids' begins to be passed round and its significance realised that people start to take notice, some at the back even standing up to get a better view of this unlikely herald.

It takes a little time and while there is some shaking of heads at first, soon smiles begin to break out, people perk up and this nondescript young man suddenly finds himself addressing an audience that hangs on his every word. 'I know there is nothing to be ashamed of whatever it was he died of, but with all due respect to the person who spoke, who obviously knew him much better than I did, all the same I was there

69

when he died and I'm sure his aunt, at least, would like to know it was not Aids.'

'HIV-related,' corrected a man with a ponytail.

'Yes, whatever,' says the student.

'It wasn't Aids,' Miss Wishart's helpful neighbour shouts in her ear. 'Not Aids.'

Meeting an uncomprehending smile from the old lady, she thinks to mime the condition by pointing to her bottom and shaking her head, thereby causing much offence to Carl and his glabrous colleagues and bringing Miss Wishart no nearer enlightenment. The only aids she has come across are deaf aids and hers plainly isn't working.

Hopkins, having given his welcome news, offers no evidence to back it up and now seems disposed to sit down again except that Father Jolliffe, who, if he had been an MP and addressing the House of Commons, would at this point have had to preface his question by declaring an interest, leans over the lectern and says, 'And do you mind telling us Mr . . . ?'

'Hopkins.'

'Mr Hopkins, do you mind telling us how Mr Dunlop did die?'

The young man blew his nose, carefully wiped it, and put away his handkerchief.

'Well, basically he had been on a trip which took him through some rough country where he was like bitten by some insect or other, you know, the name of which I can't remember, only the doctors at the hospital knew it. He got this fever. He was in the room next door to me at the hotel, to begin with anyway. Then they took him in and that was it basically. I was surprised as it's not a tropical place. The climate's not very different from Sheffield. I come from Sheffield,' he added apologetically.

Hopkins remained on his feet looking round at the congregation and smiling helpfully as if to suggest that if there were any more questions he would be happy to try and answer them. He doesn't have long to wait.

'I do not believe this,' Carl mutters as he gets to his feet though it is not to ask a question. He wholly ignores the student and talks to the church. 'I'm sorry? I thought we'd grown up? I thought we'd learned to look this thing in the face? I never thought I'd still be hearing tales of some ailment picked up in the wilds of Tibet. Or a wasting disease caught from the udders of Nepalese yaks. It's not from a bite. It's not from cat hairs. It's not from poppers nor is it a congenital disease of the dick. It's a virus passed via blood and sex and that's how it's caught. Not from some fucking Peruvian caterpillar. Of course it was Aids. Look at his life. How could it be anything else?'

In the silence that followed, many look desperately at the student in the hope he has something more to offer by way of rebuttal. But at 19 debate is hardly his strong point. He shrugs awkwardly and sits down shaking his head, long wrists dangling between his knees.

Unpleasant and arrogant though Carl had been, and with a manner seemingly designed to put people's backs up, there were many in the congregation who felt that he was right. They longed passionately to believe in this Peruvian caterpillar and its death-dealing bite. South America was a dangerous place, everyone knew that; there were the pampas, gauchos and regular revolutions. The Maya had perished, so why not Clive? But what Carl had said made sense. Of course it was Aids. No one could screw as much as he had done and go unpunished. So the sentence that had been all too briefly remitted was now reimposed and hopes momentarily raised were dashed once more. But to have been given a vision of peace of mind and then to see it snatched away made the burden even harder to bear.

One couple held each other's hands in mute misery. Which had slept with Clive – or both? What did it matter? Never had they been so close.

Still, the couples who had shared Clive's favours were better placed than husbands or wives who had known him singly. 'What does it signify anyway,' said a fierce-eyebrowed judge, to whom Clive was only someone who occasionally unfroze his shoulder. 'He's dead, that's the essence of it.' His wife, who was keeping very quiet, shifted in her seat slightly as she was suffering from thrush, or that was what she hoped.

Symptoms were back generally. A pitiless quiz-show host found herself with a dry mouth. The suffragan bishop knew he had a rash. A stand-up comedian had a cold sore that didn't seem to clear up and which was masked by make-up. Now it had suddenly begun to itch. He had a powder compact but dared not consult it. Those who were famous, though, knew better than to turn a hair. Their anxiety must be kept private and unshown for they were always under scrutiny. They must wait to share their worries discreetly with friends or, if with the general public, at a decent price from the newspapers concerned.

Husbands who thought their wives didn't know, put a face on it (though their wives did know very often). Wives who thought their husbands didn't know (which they generally didn't) masked their distraction in a show of concern for others, one, for instance, patting the shoulder of a man in front who, without looking, took the hand and held it to his cheek.

The congregation had been given a glimpse of peace; the itch had gone, the cough had stilled, the linen was unsoiled; the pores had closed, the pus dried up and the stream ran clear and cool. But that was what it had been, a glimpse only. Now there was to be no healing. There was only faith.

How to put this into prayer. Father Jolliffe

clasped his hands and tried once more. 'Shall we pray.'

They settled and waited as he sought for the words.

'May I speak?'

Baulked for a second unbelievable time on the brink of intercession, Father Jolliffe nearly said 'No' (which is what the Archdeacon would have said, who has long since written down: 'Hopeless. Lacks grip.' And now inserts 'totally').

Father Jolliffe searches the congregation to see who it is who has spoken and sees, standing at the back, a tall, distinguished-looking man. 'I am a doctor,' he says.

This is unsurprising because it is just what he looks like. He is dry, kindly-faced and yet another one who doesn't speak up. 'I am a doctor,' he repeats. 'Mr Dunlop's doctor, in fact. While his medical history must, of course, be confidential' – 'Must be what?' somebody says. 'Controversial,' says someone else – 'I think I am not breaking any rules when I say that Mr Dunlop was a most . . . ah . . . responsible patient and came to me over a period of years for regular blood tests.'

'Regular blood tests,' goes round the pews.

'These were generally a propos HIV, the last one only a week before his departure for South America. It was negative. What this fever was that he died of I'm in no position to say, but contrary to the assertions made by the gentleman who spoke earlier' – he meant Carl – 'it seems to me most unlikely, in fact virtually impossible, that it was HIV-related. Still,' he smiled sadly, 'the fact remains that Clive is dead and I can only offer my condolences to his grieving friends and to his aunt. Whatever it was her nephew died of, her grief must be unchanged.'

Miss Wishart is nudged by her neighbour and when the doctor is pointed out to her, smiles happily and gives him a little wave. She seldom got such a good ride as this.

As the doctor sat down there was a ripple of applause and as the news filtered to the acoustically disadvantaged areas of the church it grew and grew. People at the front stood up and began applauding louder and those further back followed suit until the whole church was on its feet clapping.

'Good old Clive!' someone shouted.

'Trust Clive,' said someone else and there was

even some of that overhead clapping and wild whoops that nowadays characterises audiences in a TV studio or at a fashionable first night.

Seldom even at a wedding had the vicar seen so many happy faces, some openly laughing, some weeping even and many of them embracing one another as they were called on to do in the Communion Service, but never with a fervour or a fellow-feeling so unembarrassed as this. It was, thought Father Jolliffe, just as it should be.

Still, it was hard to say what it was they were applauding: Clive for having died of the right thing (or not having died of the wrong one) and for having been so sensible about his blood tests; the young student for having brought home the news; or the urbane-looking doctor for having confirmed it. Father Jolliffe was glad to see that God came in for some of the credit and mindful of the setting one woman sank to her knees in prayer, and both genders got onto their mobiles to relay the news to partners and friends whose concern for themselves (and for Clive, of course) was as keen as those present in the congregation.

Some wept and, seeing the tears, wondering partners took them as tears for Clive. But funeral tears seldom flow for anyone other than the person crying them and so it was here. They cried for Clive, it is true, but they cried for themselves without Clive, particularly now that his clean and uncomplicated death meant that he had thankfully left them with nothing to remember him by.

Amid the general rejoicing even Carl looked a little more cheerful, though it was hard for him to be altogether wholehearted, the dead man just having been dropped from a club of which Carl was still a life member and from which he stood no chance of exclusion. There were one or two others in the same boat and knew it, but they clapped too, and tried to rejoice.

Though his companion the novelist was gratefully weeping, the publisher's thanksgiving was less wholehearted. Aids never did sales any harm and gave a tragic momentum even to the silliest of lives, whereas it was hard not to think that there was only bathos in a death that resulted from being bitten by a caterpillar. Still, the geology student seemed naive and possibly

suggestible, so Clive's death could be made –
and moralistically speaking ought to be made –
more ambiguous than it really was. Nobody
liked someone who had had as much sex as
Clive to get off scot free and that included the
idle reader. No, there was a book here even so;
the absurd death was just a hiccup and smiling
too, the publisher joined in the clapping.

But clapping whom? Father Jolliffe decided it
might as well be God and raising his voice above
the tumult he said: 'Now (and for the third time
of asking), shall we pray?' This even got a laugh
and there was a last whoop before the congregation settled down. 'Let us in the silence remember our friend Clive, who is dead but is alive
again.'

This, however hallowed, was not just a
phrase. Clive's imagined death had been baneful
and fraught with far-reaching implications so
that, devoid of these, his real (and more salubri-
ous) demise did seem almost a resurrection.
And in that cumbrous silence, laden with
prayers unmouthed, loosed from anxiety and
recrimination many do now try and remember
him, some frowning as they pray with eyes

closed but seeing him still, some open-eyed but unseeing of the present, lost in recollection. In the nature of things, these memories are often inappropriate. Some think, for instance, of what Clive felt like, smelled like, recalling his tenderness and his tact. There was the diligence of his application and pictured in more than one mind's eye was that stern and labouring face rising and falling in the conscientious performance of his professional duties.

'I sing his body,' prayed Geoffrey to himself. 'I sing his marble back, his heavy legs' – he had been reading Whitman – 'I sing the absence of preliminaries, the curtness of desire. Dead, but not ominously so, now I extol him.'

'I elevate him,' thought a choreographer (for whom he had also made some shelves), 'a son of Job dancing before the Lord.'

'I dine him,' prayed one of the cooks, 'on quails stuffed with pears in a redcurrant coulis.'

'I adorn him,' imagined a fashion designer. 'I send him down the catwalk in chest-revealing tartan tunic and trews and sporting a tam o'shanter.'

'I appropriate him,' planned the publisher, 'a

young man eaten alive by celebrity' (the dust-jacket Prometheus on the rock).

None, though, thought of words and how the bedroom had been Clive's education. It was there that he learned that words mattered, once having been in bed with an etymologist whose ejaculation had been indefinitely postponed when Clive (on being asked if he was about to come too) had murmured, 'Hopefully.' In lieu of discharge, the etymologist had poured his frustrated energy into a short lecture on neologisms which Clive had taken so much to heart he had never said 'hopefully' again.

Nothing surprised him, nothing shocked him. He was not – the word nowadays would be judgmental, but Clive knew that there were some who disliked this word, too, and preferred censorious, but he was not judgmental of that either.

Words mattered and so did names. He knew if someone disliked their name and did not want it said, still less called out, during lovemaking. He knew, too, his clients' various names for the private parts and what he or she preferred to call them and what they preferred him to call them (which was not always the same thing). He knew, too, in the heightened atmosphere of the bedroom how swiftly a misappellation in this regard could puncture desire and shrivel its manifestation.

He brought to the bedroom a power of recall and a grasp of detail that would have taken him to the top of any profession he had chosen to enter. A man who could after several months' interval recall which breast his client preferred caressed could have run the National Theatre or reformed the Stock Exchange. He knew what stories to whisper and when not to tell stories at all and knew, too, when the business was over, never to make reference to what had been said.

Put simply this was a man who had learned never to strike a false note. He was a professional.

Aloud Geoffrey said: 'Let us magnify him before the Lord. O all ye works of the Lord, bless ye the Lord: praise him and magnify him for ever.'

Geoffrey rose to his feet. 'And now we end this service of thanksgiving with John Keble's hymn.'

New every morning is the love . . .
Our waking and uprising prove
Through sleep and darkness safely brought
Restored to life and power and thought.

How glumly they had come into the church and how happily now, their burden laid down, do they prepare to go forth. So they sing this mild little hymn as the chorus sings their deliverance in *Fidelio*, or the crowd sings at Elland Road. They sing, distasteful though that spectacle often is, as they sing at the Last Night of the Proms. And singing they are full of new resolve.

Since the news of Clive's death a shadow had fallen across sexual intercourse. Coming together had become wary, the whole business perfunctory and self-serving, and even new relationships had been entered on gingerly. As one wife, not in the know, had complained, 'There is no giving any more.' In some bedrooms where intercourse had not been wholly discontinued prophylactics had appeared for the first time, variously explained by a trivial infection or a sudden sensitivity, but in all cases made out to the unknowing partner as just a minor precaution not the membrane between life and death.

Now that time of sexual austerity was over. This was the liberation, and many of the couples pressing out of the door looked forward to resuming all those sexually sophisticated manoeuvres that Clive's death and its presumed cause had seen discontinued.

Partners not in the know were taken aback by the gusto with which their long-diffident opposites now went to it, and some, to put it plainly, could scarcely wait to get home in order to have a fuck. And indeed some didn't, one couple sneaking round behind the church to the alcove outside the vestry that sheltered the dustbins and doing it there. They happened both to be friends of Clive and so of the same mind, but several husbands, ignorant of their wives' connection with the dead man, were startled to find themselves unexpectedly fingered and fondled (evidence of the strong tide of relief that was sweeping their partners along) and one, made to park on a double yellow line in the Goswell Road, had to spread a copy of the *Financial Times* over his knees while beneath it his wife gave vent to her euphoria.

For some, though, deliverance would be all

too brief. A TV designer, a particular friend of Clive and thus feeling himself more en-shadowed than most, was so rapturous at the news of Clive's unportentous death that he celebrated by picking up a dubious young man in Covent Garden, spending a delightful evening and an unprotected night, waking the next morning as anxious as he had been before and in much the same boat.

Still, others thought they had learned their lesson and crowding up the aisles they saw the west door open on a churchyard now bathed in sunlight. The bells were ringing out; the vicar was there shaking hands; truly this had been a thanksgiving and an ending and now the portals were flung open on a new life.

'I presume he had us all on his computer somewhere,' someone said.

'Who cares?' said someone else.

Slowly they shuffled towards the light.

IT WAS NOW well past lunchtime and the Archdeacon had stomach ache. Anxious to get away before the crowd and unobserved by the vicar, who would surely be shaking all those famous hands, Canon Treacher had got up smartly after the blessing only to find his exit from the pew blocked by a woman doing what she (and Canon Treacher) had been brought up to do, namely, on entering or leaving a church to say a private prayer. It was all Treacher could do not to step over her, but instead waited there fuming while she placidly prayed. She took her time with God, and then, her devotions ended, more time assembling her umbrella, gloves and what she called apologetically 'my bits and bobs' and then when she was finally ready, had to turn back to retrieve her Order of Service, which she held up at Canon Treacher with a brave smile as if to signify that this had been a job well done. By which time, of course, the aisle was clogged with people and Treacher found himself carried slowly but inexorably towards the door where, as he had feared, Father Jolliffe was now busy shaking hands.

Even so, the priest was so deep in conversation with a leading chat-show host that Treacher thought he was going to manage to sidle by unnoticed. Except that then the priest saw him and the chat-show host, used to calling the shots with regard to when conversations began and ended, was startled to find this chat abruptly wound up as Jolliffe hastened across to shake Treacher's cold, withdrawing hand.

'Archdeacon. What a pleasure to see you. Did you know Clive?'

'Who? Certainly not. How should I know him?'

'He touched life at many points.'

It was a joke but Treacher did not smile.

'Not at this one.'

'And did you enjoy the service?' Father Jolliffe's plump face was full of pathetic hope.

Treacher smiled thinly but did not yield. 'It was . . . interesting.'

With Father Jolliffe cringing under the archidiaconal disapproval it ought to have been a chilling moment and, by Treacher at least, savoured and briefly enjoyed, but it was muffed when the hostess of a rapid response TV cookery show, whom the vicar did not know, suddenly flung her arms round his neck saying, 'Oh, pumpkin!'

Firm in the culinary grasp, Father Jol liffe gazed helplessly as the Archdeacon was borne away on the slow-moving tide and out into the chattering churchyard where, holy ground notwithstanding, Treacher noted that many of the congregation were already feverishly lighting up.

When, a few days later, Treacher delivered his report, it was not favourable, which saddened the Bishop (who had, though it's of no relevance, been a great hurdler in his day). Rather mischievously he asked Treacher if he had nevertheless managed to enjoy the service.

'I thought it,' said Treacher, 'a useful lesson in the necessity for ritual. Or at any rate, form. Ritual is a road, a path between hedges, a track along which the priest leads his congregation.'

'Yes,' said the Bishop, who had been here before.

'Leave the gate open, nay tell them it's open as this foolish young man did, and straightaway they're through it, trampling everything underfoot.'

'You make the congregation sound like cattle, Arthur.'

'No, not cattle, Bishop. Sheep, a metaphor for which there is some well-known authority in scripture. It was a scrum. A free-for-all.'

'Yes,' said the Bishop. 'Still,' he smiled wistfully, 'That gardening girl, the footballer who's always so polite – I quite wish I'd been there.'

Treacher, feeling unwell, now passes out of this narrative, though with more sympathy and indeed regret than his acerbities might seem to warrant. Though he had disapproved of the memorial service and its altogether too heartfelt antics he is not entirely to be deplored, standing in this story for dignity, formality and self-restraint.

Less feeling was what Treacher wanted, the services of the church, as he saw it, a refuge from the prevailing sloppiness. As opportunities multiplied for the display of sentiment in public and on television – confessing, grieving and giving way to anger, and always with a ready access to tears – so it seemed to Treacher that there was needed a place for dryness and self-control and this was the church. It was not a popular view and he sometimes felt that he had much in common with a Jesuit priest on the run in Elizabethan England – clandestine, subversive and holding to the old faith, even though the tenets of that faith, discretion, understatement and respect for tradition, might seem more suited to tailoring than they did to religion.

Once out of the churchyard the Archdeacon lit up, his smoking further evidence that there was more to this man than has been told in this tale. There had briefly been a Mrs Treacher, a nice woman but she had died. He would die soon, too, and the Bishop at least would be relieved.

BACK at the church, Geoffrey was shaking hands to the finish, with last out, as always, Miss Wishart who was still attesting her supposed connection with the deceased. 'Somebody said something about drinks for my nephew. Where would they be? A sherry was what he preferred only I like wine.'

The priest pointed her vaguely in the direction of the churchyard which with people standing about talking and laughing looked like a cocktail party anyway. He had been asked to drinks himself by a florid and effusive character, a publisher apparently, with a stony-faced woman in tow. He had taken both Geoffrey's hands warmly in his, saying he had this brilliant idea for a book and he wanted to run it past him.

This, taken with the upbeat conclusion of the service, ought to have cheered him, but Father Jolliffe found himself despondent. The presence of the Archdeacon could only mean one thing: he had been vetted. For what he wasn't sure, but for promotion certainly. And equally certainly he had failed to impress. For a start he should not have invited the congregation to participate. He knew that from something that had happened at the Board, when in answer to a question about the kiss of peace and the degree of conviviality acceptable at the Eucharist, he had said that the priest was, in a real sense, the master of ceremonies. This had got a laugh from the Board (the Bishop actually guffawing), except that he had noticed that Treacher was smiling in a different way and making one of his spidery notes: he was not impressed then and he had not been impressed now.

Still had he not, as it were, thrown the service open to the floor, the true circumstances of Clive's death would never have emerged so he could not regret that. What the Lord giveth the

Lord also taketh away. He went back into the now empty church to get out of his gear.

'SHOULD I have spoken?' Hopkins was still slumped in his pew. Now he got up clutching his backpack in front of him like a shield. 'I wondered if it was out of turn.'

'Not at all,' said Geoffrey, noticing that the young man had loosened the unaccustomed tie and undone the top button of his shirt, so that he looked younger still and not so old-fashioned. It was difficult to think of him at Clive's death-bed.

'You did the right thing, Mr Hopkins. There were many people' – he didn't say himself – 'who were grateful. It lifted a burden.'

The boy sat down again cradling his backpack. 'The young guy seemed pretty pissed off. The – ' he hesitated, 'the gay one?'

Hopkins had an unconvincing earring that Geoffrey had not spotted, ear and earring now briefly caught in a shaft of light, a faint fuzz on the fresh pink ear.

'People were upset,' Geoffrey said. 'Clive was . . . well, Clive.' He smiled, but the young man still looked unhappy.

'I felt a fool.' He sat hugging his backpack then suddenly brightened up. 'That blonde from *EastEnders* was on my row. Clive never told me he knew her.'

Geoffrey thought that there were probably quite a few things Clive had never told him and wondered if anything had happened between them. Probably not, if only because he imagined there was more on offer in South America and the local talent doubtless more exotic.

He was an awkward boy with big hands. He was the kind of youth Modigliani painted and for a moment Geoffrey wondered if he was attractive, but decided he was just young.

'And that cook who slags people off? He was here too.'

'Yes,' said Geoffrey. 'It was a good turn-out.' Then, feeling he ought to be getting on. 'They're all outside.'

The youth did not notice the hint still less take it. 'You said you knew Clive?'

'Yes,' said Geoffrey, then added, 'but not well.'

'I'd never seen anybody die before. It was depressing?'

Geoffrey smiled sadly and nodded as if this were an aspect of death that had not occurred to him. The youth was a fool.

'Can I show you something?' The student rooted in his pack then put it on the floor so that the priest could sit beside him. 'I had to go through his stuff after he died. There wasn't much. He was travelling light. Only there was this.'

It was a maroon notebook, long, cloth-covered and meant to fit easily into a pocket. Geoffrey thought he remembered it and ran his hand over the smooth, soft cover.

'Is it a diary?' the priest said.

'Not exactly.'

IN THE CHURCHYARD the party was beginning to break up. One group had arranged to lunch at the Garrick and were moving round saying their farewells while someone looked for a cab. Others were going off to investigate a new restaurant that had opened in a converted public lavatory and of which they'd heard good reports, though tempted to join forces with yet another party who were venturing into one of the last genuine cafés patronised by the porters at Smithfield where the tripe was said to be delicious.

Most of the big stars had left pretty promptly, their cars handily waiting nearby to shield them from too much unmediated attention. The pop star's limo dropped him first then called at the bank so that the security guard could redeposit the clasp and then took him on to a laboratory in Hounslow where, as a change from Catherine the Great, he was mounting vigil over some hamsters testing lip-gloss. Meanwhile, the autograph hunters moved among what was left of the congregation, picking up what dregs of celebrity that remained.

'Are you anybody?' a woman said to the partner of a soap-star, 'or are you just with him?'

'He was my nephew,' said Miss Wishart to anyone who would listen.

'Who, dear?' said one of the photographers, which of course Miss Wishart didn't hear, but she looked so forlorn he took her picture anyway, which was fortunate, as he was later able to submit it to the National Portrait Gallery where it duly featured in an exhibition alongside the stage doorman of the Haymarket and the maître d' of the Ivy as one of 'The Faces of London'.

Soon, though, it began to spit with rain and within a few minutes the churchyard was empty and after its brief bout of celebrity, back to looking as dingy and desolate as it generally did.

'NO, it isn't a diary,' said Hopkins. 'It's more of an account book.'

It was divided into columns across the page, each column numbered, possibly indicating a week or a month, the broad left-hand column a list of initials, and in the other columns figures, possibly amounts. The figures were closely packed and as neat as the work of a professional accountant.

'Can you make it out?' said the young man, running his finger down the left-hand column. 'These are people, I take it.'

'They might be,' said Geoffrey. 'I don't quite know.' Having just spotted his own initials, Geoffrey knew only too well, though he noted that the spaces opposite his own name were only occasionally filled in. This was because Clive came round quite sporadically and wasn't often available when Geoffrey called (now, seeing the number of people on his list, he could see why). When he did come round the visit did not always involve sex ('No funny business' is how Clive put it). Geoffrey told himself that this was because he was a clergyman and that he thus enjoyed a relationship with Clive that was pastoral as well as physical. More often than not this meant he found himself making Clive scrambled eggs, while Clive lay on the sofa watching TV in his underpants, which was about as close to domesticity as Geoffrey ever got. Still, Geoffrey had always insisted on paying for this privilege (hence the entries in the notebook), though really in order to give credence to the fiction that sex wasn't what their friendship was about. Though, since he was paying for it, it wasn't about friendship either, but that managed to be overlooked.

'Did you see a lot of each other? In Peru?'

Geoffrey was anxious to turn the page and get away from those incriminating initials.

'Yes. We had meals together quite often. I could never figure out what he was doing there.'

'What did you eat?' said Geoffrey. 'Eggs?'

'Beans, mostly. He said he was travelling round. Seeing the world.'

As casually as he could Geoffrey turned the page.

'These figures,' said Hopkins, turning it back. 'What do you think they mean?'

'They're on this page, too,' said Geoffrey turning the page again. 'And here,' turning another.

Hopkins blew his nose, wiped it carefully and put the handkerchief away. 'Is it sex, do you think?'

'Sex?' said Geoffrey with apparent surprise. 'Why should it be sex?' He looked at Hopkins as if the insinuation were his and almost felt sorry for him when the young geologist blushed.

'Clive was a masseur. They may be payments on account – if they're payments at all. I think when he was hard up at one period he used to provide home help, carpentry and so on. It could be that.'

'Yes? You say he was a masseur. He told me he was a writer.'

Geoffrey smiled and shook his head.

'My guess is that it's a sort of diary and I don't feel,' Geoffrey said pompously, 'that one ought to read other people's diaries, do you?'

Hopkins shrank still further and Geoffrey hated himself. He went on leafing through. Against some of the names were small hieroglyphics that seemed to denote a sexual preference or practice, an indication of a client's predilections possibly, of which one or two were obvious. Lips with a line through, for instance, must mean the person with the initials didn't like being kissed; lips with a tick the reverse. But what did a drawing of a foot indicate? Or an ear? Or (in one case) two ears?

None of the drawings was in any sense obscene and were so small and symbolic as to be uninteresting in themselves, but what they stood for – with sometimes a line-up of three or four symbols in a row – was both puzzling and intriguing.

It was a shock, therefore, for Geoffrey to turn the page and come across a note *en clair* that was both direct and naive:

> Palaces I have done it in:
> Westminster

Lambeth
Blenheim
Buckingham (2)
Windsor

Except Windsor was crossed out with a note, 'Not a palace' and an arrow led from Westminster to a bubble saying 'Lost count'. Written down baldly like this it seemed so childish and unsophisticated as not to be like Clive at all, though as notes for a book, Geoffrey could see it made some sort of sense.

'It's rather sad, really,' Geoffrey went on, still in his pompous mode. 'Why bother to write it down? Who'd be interested?'

'Oh, I keep notes myself,' said Hopkins. Then, as the priest looked up, startled, 'Oh, not about that. Just on rocks and stuff. He told me he was writing a book, but people do say that, don't they? Particularly in South America.'

It's true Clive had spoken of writing a book, or at least of being able to write a book, 'I could write a book,' often how he ended an account of some outrageous escapade. Geoffrey may even have said, 'Why don't you?' though without ever dreaming he would.

Like many who hanker after art, though, Clive

was saving it up, if not quite for a rainy day at least until the right opportunity presented itself – prison perhaps, a long illness or a spell in the back of beyond. Which, of course, Peru was and which was why, Geoffrey presumed, he had taken along the book.

Still, he wasn't sure. Clive was always so discreet and even when telling some sexual tale he seldom mentioned names and certainly not the kind of names represented at the memorial service. This iron discretion was, Clive knew, one of his selling points and part of his credit, so not an asset he was likely to squander. Or not yet anyway.

Hopkins seemed to be taking less interest in the diary and when Geoffrey closed the book and put it on the pew between them the young man did not pick it up but just sat staring into space.

Then: 'Of course, if it is sex and those are initials and you could identify them it would be dynamite.'

'Well, a mild sort of dynamite,' said Geoffrey, 'and only if a person,' Geoffrey smiled at the young man, 'only if a person was planning to reveal information . . .' He left the sentence unfinished. 'And that would, of course, be . . .' and he left this sentence unfinished too, except at that moment a police car blared past outside. Geoffrey sighed. God could be so unsubtle sometimes. 'Besides,' he went on, 'if this is entirely about sex, and I'm not sure it is, it's not against the law is it?' He wondered how long he could get away with reckoning to be so stupid.

Having found someone, as he thought, more ingenuous than himself the young man was determined to instruct him in the ways of the world. 'No,' he said patiently, 'but it would make a story. Several stories probably. Stories for which newspapers would pay a lot of money.'

'You wouldn't do that, surely?'

'I wouldn't, but someone might.' Hopkins picked up the book. 'I wondered about handing it over to the police.'

'The police?' Geoffrey found himself suddenly angry at the boy's foolishness. 'What for?'

'For safe-keeping?'

'Safe-keeping,' shouted Geoffrey, all pretence of naivety gone. 'Safe-keeping? In which case why bother with the police at all. Just cut out the middleman and give it to the *News of the World*?'

Taken aback by this unexpected outburst Hopkins looked even more unhappy. 'I don't know,' he said, nuzzling his chin on top of his pack. 'I just want to do the right thing.'

The right thing to do was nothing but Geoffrey did not say so. Instead he thought of all the people behind the initials, the troubled novelists, the tearful gardeners and stone-faced soap-stars, Clive's celebrity clientele dragged one by one into the sneering, pitiless light. Something had to be done.

He put his hand on the young man's knee.

He felt Hopkins flinch but kept his hand where he had put it, or not where he had put it, he decided subsequently, but where God had put it. Because tame and timid though such a move might seem (and to someone of Clive's sophistication, for instance, nonchalant and almost instinctive), for Geoffrey it was momentous, fraught with risk and the dread of embarrassment. He had never made such a bold gesture in his life and now he had done it without thinking and almost without feeling.

The young man was unprepossessing and altogether too awkward and angular; in the street he would not have looked at him twice. But there was his hand on the boy's knee. 'What is your name?' he said.

'Greg,' Hopkins said faintly. 'It's Greg.'

Geoffrey had no thought that the presence of his hand on the young man's knee would be the slightest bit welcome nor, judging by the look of panic on his face, was it. Greg was transfixed.

'I am wondering, Greg,' said Geoffrey, 'if we are getting this right. We are talking about what to do with this notebook when strictly speaking, *legally* speaking' – he squeezed the knee slightly – 'it has got nothing to do with us anyway.'

'No?'

'No. The notebook belongs after all, to Clive. And now to his estate. And whom does his estate belong to . . . or will do eventually?'

Hopkins shook his head.

'His only surviving relative. Miss Wishart!'

The priest loosened his grip on the knee, though lingering there for a moment as it might be preparatory to travelling further up the young man's leg. This galvanised Hopkins and he got up suddenly. Except that the priest got up too, both crammed together in the close confinement of the pew, the priest seemingly unperturbed and never leaving his face his kind, professional, priestly smile.

Hopkins was now unwise enough to put his hand on the edge of the pew. Geoffrey promptly put his hand on top of it.

'No, no,' said Hopkins.

'No what?' said Geoffrey kindly.

'No, she should keep the book.' Hopkins pulled his hand away in order to retrieve the book still lying on the seat. 'Where can I find her?'

'She comes to church. I can give it to her.' Geoffrey reached for the book and fearful that he was reaching for him too, Hopkins relinquished it without a struggle.

'I can give it to her as a relic of her nephew. The only relic really.' He stroked the book fondly and in that instant Hopkins was out of the pew and on his way to the door. But not quickly enough to avoid the priest's kindly hand pressing into the small of his back and carrying with it the awful possibility that it might move lower down.

'Yes,' Hopkins said, 'give it to her. She's the

person.' And stopping suddenly in order to put on his backpack he got rid of the hand, but then found it resting even more horribly on his midriff, so that he gave a hoarse involuntary cry before the priest lifted his hand with a bland smile, converting the gesture almost into a benediction.

'Won't she be shocked?' Hopkins said as he settled the pack on his back. 'She's an old lady.'

'No,' said Geoffrey firmly. 'And I say this, Greg, as her parish priest. It's true she's an old person but I have found the old are quite hard to shock. It's the young one has to be careful with. They are the prudes nowadays.'

Hopkins nodded. Irony and geology obviously did not mix.

'I wondered if you wanted a cup of tea?' Geoffrey stroked the side of his backpack.

'No,' he said hurriedly. 'No, I've got to be somewhere.'

Still widely smiling Geoffrey put out his hand.

They shook hands and the young man dashed out of the door and quickly across the wet gravestones, Geoffrey noting as he did so that he had that over-long and slightly bouncy stride he had always associated with flute-players, train-spotters and other such unworldly and unattractive creatures.

Something strange, though, now happened that Geoffrey would later come to see as prophetic. Or at least ominous. The boy had pulled out a knitted cap and as he stopped to put it on he saw the priest still standing there. Suddenly and unexpectedly the boy smiled and raised his hand. 'I'm sorry,' he called out, and then about to go, he stopped again. 'But thank you all the same.'

Geoffrey sat down in the nearest pew. He was trembling. After a bit he got up and went into the vestry where he opened the safe in which was kept the parish plate, the chalice (Schofield of London, 1782) and the two patens (Forbes of Bristol, 1718), each in its velvet-lined case. On the shelf below them Geoffrey put Clive's book.

OVER the following weeks Geoffrey would often open up the safe and take a peek at the book, trying to decipher Clive's cryptography and gauge the extent and nature of his activities. None of it shocked him: indeed he found the found the exercise vaguely exciting and as near to pornography as he allowed himself to come.

Whether it was thanks to the book or to that almost involuntary pass that had allowed him to retain it Geoffrey found his life changing. Disappointed of immediate promotion he was now more . . . well, relaxed and though 'Relax!' is hardly at the core of the Christian message he did feel himself better for it.

So it might be because he was easier with himself or that his unique pass at the geology student had broken his duck and given him more nerve but one way and another he found himself having the occasional fling, in particular with the bus-driving crucifer, who, married though he was, didn't see that as a problem. Nor did Geoffrey's confessor who, while absolving him of what sin there was, urged him to see this and any similar experiences less as deviations from the straight and narrow and more as part of a learning curve. In fairness, this wasn't an expression Geoffrey much cared for, though he didn't demur. He preferred to think of it, if only to himself, as grace.

He still kept the book in the safe, though, as it

represented a valorous life he would have liked to lead and still found exciting. It happened that he had been to confession the day before and just as a diabetic whose blood tests have been encouraging sneaks a forbidden pastry so he felt he deserved a treat and went along to the church meaning to take out Clive's book. It was partly to revisit his memory but also because even though he now knew its mysterious notations by heart they still gave him a faint erotic thrill. He knew that this was pathetic and could have told it to no one, except perhaps Clive, and it was one of the ways he missed him.

Pushing open the door of the church he saw someone sitting towards the front and on the side. It was the geology student, slumped in the same pew he had sat in at the memorial service.

'Hail,' said the young man. 'We meet again.' Geoffrey shook hands.

'I meant to come before now,' he said, 'only my car's not been well.'

Geoffrey managed a smile. Seeing him again, Geoffrey thought how fortunate it was that his advance had been rejected. God had been kind. It would never have done.

Hopkins made room for Geoffrey to sit down, just as he had on the first occasion they had talked.

'I came back,' he said, as if it were only that morning he had fled the church. 'I thought about it and I thought, why not?' And now he turned towards Geoffrey and looking him sternly in the eye put his hand on the vicar's knee. 'All right?'

Geoffrey did not speak.

There was a click, then another and the turning of a wheel and faintly, as if from a great way off, Geoffrey heard the cogs begin to grind as the clock gathered itself up and struck the hour.

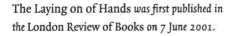

The Laying on of Hands was first published in
the London Review of Books on 7 June 2001.

The London Review of Books can be ordered
through your local newsagent or taken on subscription.
For subscriptions please call our 24-hour freephone on
0800 018 5803 (within the UK). Otherwise,
ring 020 7209 1141, fax 020 7209 1151
or e-mail subs@lrb.co.uk.